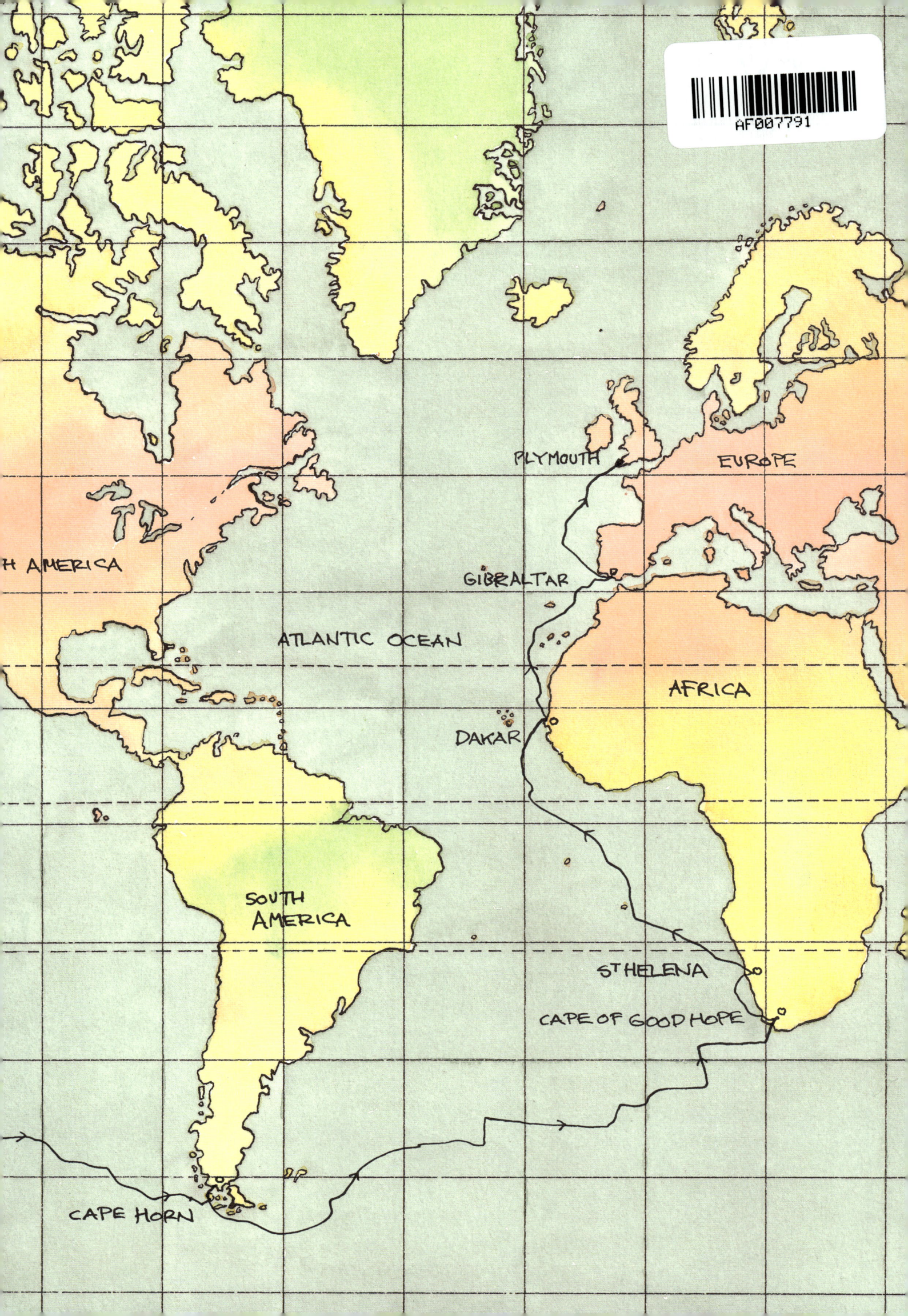

MARK GREENWOOD
TERRY DENTON

BOOMERANG AND BAT

ALLEN&UNWIN
SYDNEY·MELBOURNE·AUCKLAND·LONDON

Johnny was watching the settlers play a curious game called cricket.

'Chuck it back,' they shouted, when the ball scooted his way.

The boss at Mullagh Station invited Johnny to join in. He hit the ball so hard he split the redgum bat.

Johnny Mullagh's real name was Unaarrimin. On days off from his work as a shearer, he hunted with other station hands on the shores of Lake Wallace.

One day, he showed them a cricket bat and ball.

'Wanna play a game?' he asked. Sundown and Tiger were willing and Mosquito said he'd give it a go.

As it turned out, the station hands were natural sportsmen.

Cuzens was a fiery barefoot bowler.

Bullocky slogged cricket balls over tall trees.

After regular practice, they challenged settler teams, and won.

Their reputation grew. Before long, they were invited to play in the big city.

Johnny's batting thrilled the crowd. 'Bravo, Mullagh,' rang out across the Melbourne Cricket Ground.

That night, Johnny Mullagh and his men were presented to a cheering audience at the opera. Watching on was an English cricketer.

'If I could coach them,' thought Charles Lawrence, 'I might make a fortune.'

Backstage, he proposed a tour of England.

'I'll match you against the best cricketers in the world,' he said.

But the Board for the Protection of Aborigines objected to the team leaving the colony. 'These men might not survive the voyage,' they wrote. 'Their lives should not be put in danger.'

Charles Lawrence refused to give up. He followed the cricketers back to their stations and taught them the finer points of batting and round-arm bowling.

He encouraged spear-throwing and boomerang tricks.

After months of practice, the team made plans to leave Australia, in defiance of the authorities.

In steady, soaking rain they set off for the coast, on the first stage of their secret journey.

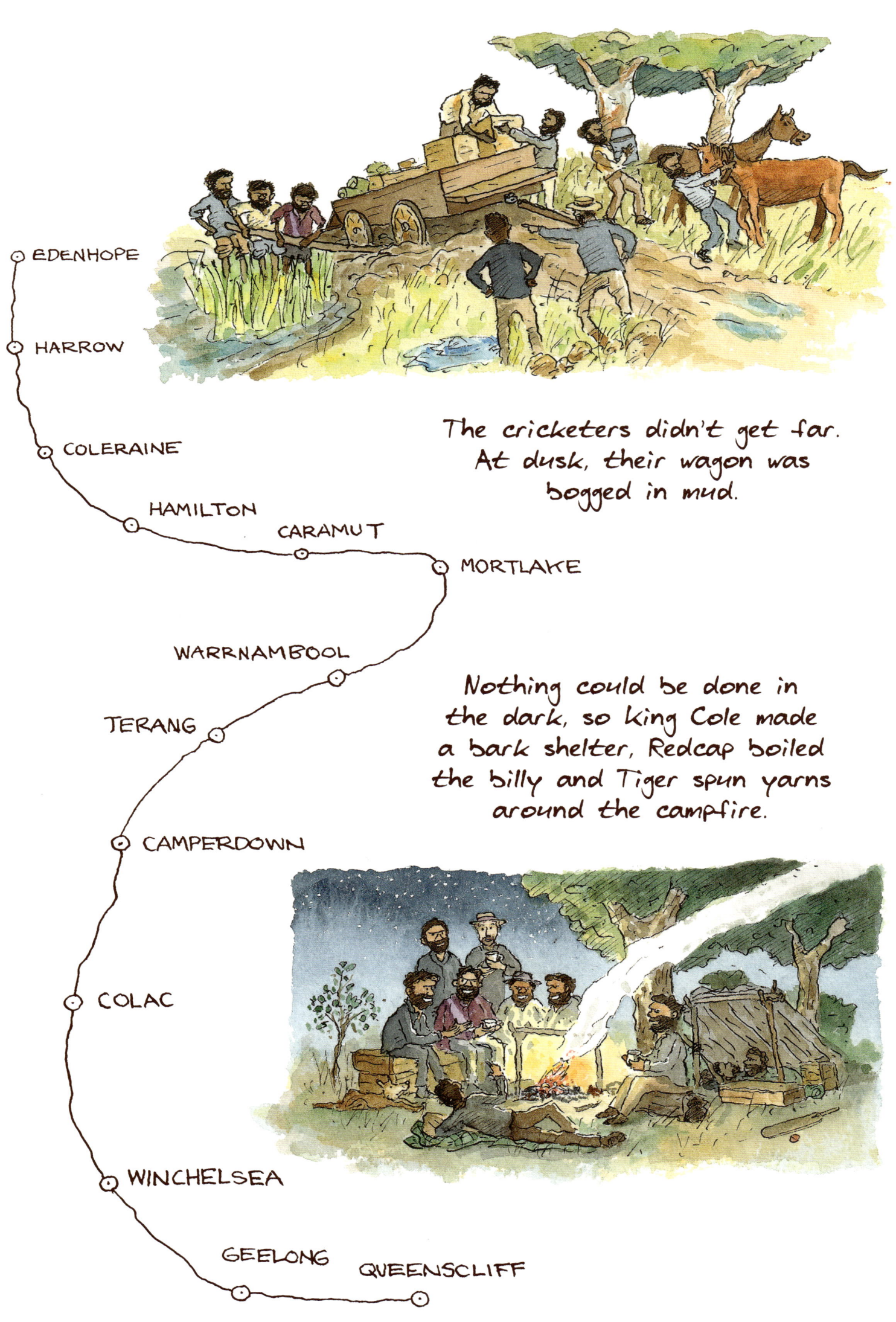

At dawn, everyone pitched in to free the wagon. Cuzens took the reins, and the horses were soon at full trot.

It took eight days to reach the coast. A longboat ferried them out to a steamer bound for Sydney. There, under cover of darkness, Charles Lawrence smuggled the team aboard a fully rigged clipper.

The Parramatta sailed south, through fields of ice.
It creaked and rolled across the vast ocean.
Tiger feared the ship might sink.

'I'm sick of the sea,' moaned Redcap.

Charley passed the time playing checkers
and Bullocky carved wooden wallabies
for the children aboard.

After three months, they finally reached England. Johnny led the team down the gangplank and they travelled by coach to Kent.

In the days that followed, crowds flocked to their training sessions. Critics predicted the visitors would be easily outclassed by English cricketers.

Polite applause welcomed the Australians to their first match. The Gentlemen of Surrey won the toss and elected to bat.

Thwaack! A contest was underway.

Johnny bowled with unpredictable swing and King Cole took a remarkable one-handed catch.

At the fall of each English wicket, Sundown celebrated with backflips and somersaults.

Johnny Mullagh top-scored with a dashing 73. The crowd rushed the field and carried him off on their shoulders.

Trains whizzed the team across England. Children scrambled for a glimpse as the cricketers steamed by.

At the close of each day's play, the team staged a spectacular show with boomerangs and spears.

With a flick of his rawhide whip, Mosquito snatched a sovereign held between a gentleman's finger and thumb.

Dick-a-Dick challenged the crowd to hurl cricket balls at him.

'Miss me,' he said, 'and I'll keep your shilling.'

The team's fame grew. At Lords, Johnny Mullagh attacked fast-rising balls with glances, cuts and cover drives.

Earls and viscounts gave him a standing ovation.

'I've never seen a finer batsman,' said a bowler on the day.

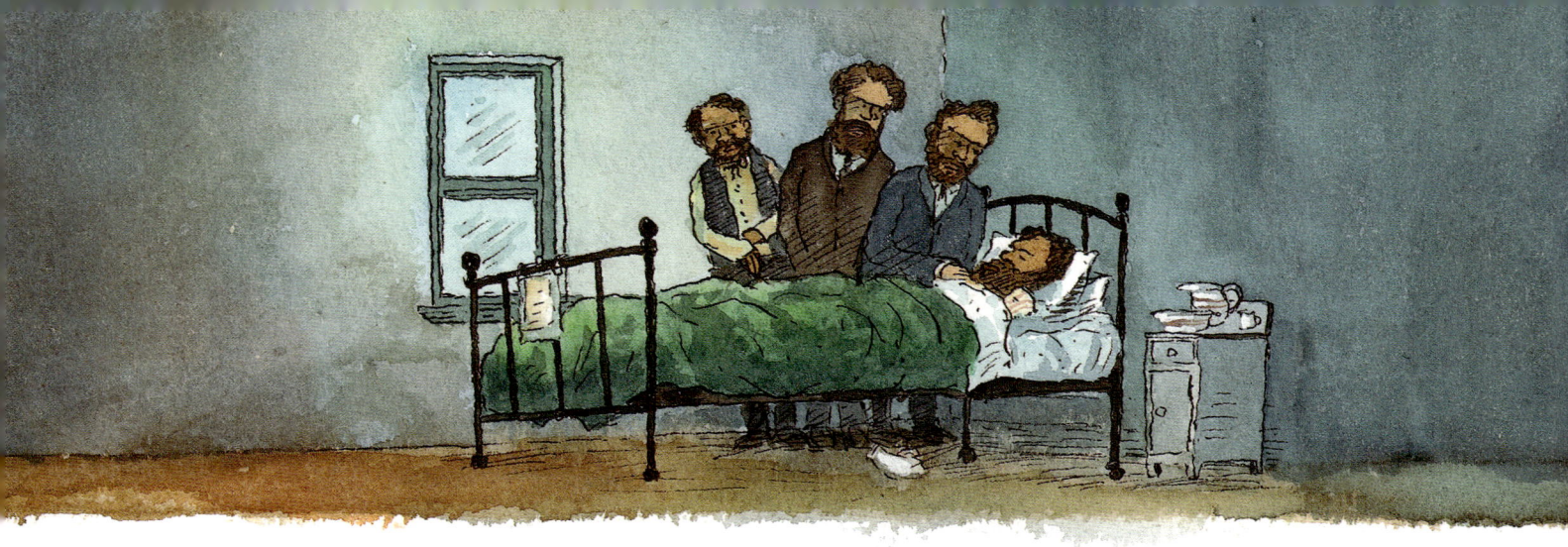

But months of non-stop touring began to take their toll. Back at their lodgings, King Cole coughed all night. The players comforted their friend. At daybreak he was taken to hospital.

The tired team played on – from Hastings to Halifax, Newcastle to Southampton.

At York they were denied service in the luncheon tent.
'Some people got no manners,' said Cuzens.

Johnny Mullagh took offence and refused to play.
'This day,' he said, 'or the next.'

Then they heard the news that King Cole had died.
Everyone was choked by sorrow.

'We're sick for our country,' said Johnny.

After forty-seven matches, the weary cricketers declared their final innings and boarded a ship bound for Australia.

There was no triumphant welcome after the long voyage home.

One by one, the cricketers quietly returned to their stations.

Johnny Mullagh continued to play the game he loved. When he appeared at local cricket matches, he often scored a hundred runs.

In memory of Bripumyarrimin (King Cole)

SPECIAL THANKS TO Jon Astley, Trevor Ruddell — assistant librarian, Melbourne Cricket Club, Angela Newton and staff at the Johnny Mullagh Interpretive Cricket Centre, David and Lou Edgar, David Wells, Curator — Bradman Foundation, Neil Robinson, Research Officer — MCC, Heather Thomas, Collections Assistant — MCC, Sean Gorman, Anne Davies and Bob Reece.

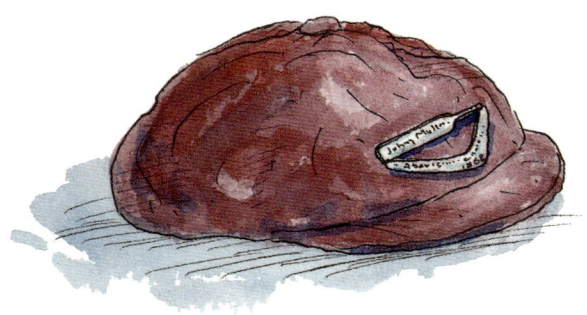

First published in 2016
Copyright © Text, Mark Greenwood 2016
Copyright © Illustrations, Terry Denton 2016

The moral right of Mark Greenwood and Terry Denton to be identified as the author and illustrator of this work has been asserted by them in accordance with the United Kingdom's *Copyright, Designs and Patents Act 1988*.

All rights reserved. No part of this book may be reproduced or transmitted in any form or by any means, electronic or mechanical, including photocopying, recording or by any information storage and retrieval system, without prior permission in writing from the publisher. The Australian *Copyright Act 1968* (the Act) allows a maximum of one chapter or ten per cent of this book, whichever is the greater, to be photocopied by any educational institution for its educational purposes provided that the educational institution (or body that administers it) has given a remuneration notice to Copyright Agency Limited (CAL) under the Act.

Allen & Unwin
83 Alexander Street
Crows Nest NSW 2065
Australia
Phone: (61 2) 8425 0100
Fax: (61 2) 9906 2218
Email: info@allenandunwin.com
Web: www.allenandunwin.com

Allen & Unwin – UK
Ormond House, 26–27 Boswell Street,
London WC1N 3JZ, UK

A Cataloguing-in-Publication entry is available from the National Library of Australia www.trove.nla.gov.au. A catalogue record for this book is available from the British Library

ISBN (AUS) 978 1 74331 924 6
ISBN (UK) 978 1 74336 833 6

Teachers' notes available from www.allenandunwin.com

Cover and text design by Terry Denton and Ruth Grüner
Set in 16 pt blzee by Ruth Grüner
The illustrations for this book were done using pencil, pen and (india) ink and watercolour on Arches paper.
Colour reproduction by Splitting Image, Clayton, Victoria
This book was printed in January 2016 at Hang Tai Printing (Guang Dong) Ltd, China

1 3 5 7 9 10 8 6 4 2

Zellanach
JOHNNY CUZENS
Fiery fast bowler

Bullchanach
HARRY BULLOCKY
Wicketkeeper

Jumgumjenanuke
DICK-A-DICK
Expert at dodging cricket balls

Unaarrimin
JOHNNY MULLAGH
Outstanding all-round cricketer

Pripumuarraman
CHARLEY DUMAS
Batsman and boomerang thrower

Bonnibarnjeet
TIGER
Batted in all tour matches

Lytejerbillijun
JIM CROW
Batsman and spear thrower